STAR WARS™
WHERE'S THE WOOKIEE? 2

EGMONT
We bring stories to life

First published in Great Britain 2017 by Egmont UK Limited
The Yellow Building, 1 Nicholas Road, London W11 4AN

Illustrations by Ulises Farinas
Colour by Gabriel Cassata
Written by Katrina Pallant
Designed by Richie Hull

© & ™ 2017 Lucasfilm Ltd.
ISBN 978 1 4052 8418 9
62260/5
Printed in Italy

To find more great *Star Wars* books, visit www.egmont.co.uk/starwars

WULLFFWARRO

TARFFUL

BLACK KRRSANTAN

CHEWBACCA

GUNGI

CHALPAL

FIND THIS WOOKIEE!

Chewbacca is hiding in every location. But watch out! Decoy Wookiees are also out and about. See how many of these hairy giants are in each location.

RORJOW

CHALKAZZA

LOHGARRA

ULIBACCA

LOCATIONS

RAARRWWR ARARRRRR

Chewbacca is back and this time he has brought some Wookiee friends. The hairy hero has been spotted across the galaxy joined by rebel allies for you to find. But beware! The following locations also hide enemies from the Empire and First Order.

KAMINO CLONING FACILITY

DROID FACTORY

OTOH GUNGA

LOTHAL

DOCKING BAY 94

THE PIT OF CARKOON

HOME ONE

JEDHA

SAW GERRERA'S HIDEOUT

SCARIF

NIIMA OUTPOST

THE *ERAVANA*

MAZ KANATA'S CASTLE

STARKILLER BASE

RESISTANCE BASE

KAMINO CLONING FACILITY

On an aquatic planet south of the Rishi Maze lives a tall, elegant race called the Kaminoans. They are well known for their cloning technology and are tasked with building an army vitally important to the Galactic Republic.

OBI-WAN KENOBI | **99** | **ASAJJ VENTRESS** | **GENERAL GRIEVOUS** | **JANGO FETT** | **YOUNG BOBA FETT**

DROID FACTORY

The Geonosians are a technologically advanced species, making their homeworld an ideal place for a massive battle droid foundry. Each facility houses hundreds of conveyor belts capable of creating thousands of droids a day.

COUNT DOOKU | POGGLE THE LESSER | R2-D2 | C-3PO | WAT TAMBOR | SHU MAI

OTOH GUNGA

Beneath the waters of Naboo lies a city of bubbles; a series of buildings created by the amphibious Gungans. They are a proud warrior race that, despite their peaceful nature, would do anything to protect their home.

JAR JAR BINKS | PADMÉ AMIDALA | RISH LOO | AHSOKA | ANAKIN SKYWALKER | BOSS NASS

LOTHAL

A planet in the Outer Rim territories, Lothal was in such economic hardship that its people invited the Empire with open arms. Now disillusioned with their oppressors, some Lothalites welcome the appearance of rebel cells, black-market activity and all-out resistance to the Imperial regime.

HERA   EZRA   KANAN   SABINE   INQUISITOR   CHOPPER

DOCKING BAY 94

The *Millennium Falcon* can frequently be seen in the spaceport of Mos Eisley, where smuggling jobs can easily be found. The pilot Han Solo docks his beloved freighter here to enjoy the port's entertainment and pick up new business, but also has to dodge his disgruntled former employers.

KABE GREEDO GARINDAN PONDA BABA MOMAW NADON MUFTAK

THE PIT OF CARKOON

In the desert of Tatooine lies a giant pit, which is home to a terrifying creature known as the sarlacc. Crime lord Jabba the Hutt uses the pit to frighten his enemies and frequently visits it aboard his sail barge, the *Khetanna*.

| HAN SOLO | BOBA FETT | BIB FORTUNA | BOUSHH | MAX REBO | EV-9D9 |

HOME ONE

Home One was originally built to explore deep space, but now serves as a military vessel and is armed with ion cannons, turbolasers and several tractor beams. This star cruiser is the largest and most advanced ship in the Alliance Fleet, making it a crucial base of operations for the rebel cause.

PRINCESS LEIA **GENERAL MADINE** **WEDGE ANTILLES** **2-1B** **LANDO CALRISSIAN** **NIEN NUNB**

JEDHA

This ancient desert moon is rich in kyber crystals and therefore of great significance to the Empire. Though occupied by Imperial forces, the deeply spiritual people of Jedha continue to worship the Force and welcome pilgrims to the Holy City.

SILVANIE PHEST · KULLBEE SPERADO · WEETEEF · K-2SO · BEEZER FORTUNA · MOROFF

SAW GERRERA'S HIDEOUT

Coordinating a rebellion against the occupying forces on Jedha, Saw Gerrera is a familiar face in the fight against the Empire. Now bunkered down in his secluded caves, Saw has his gang of rebels carry out brutal missions to destabilise the regime.

G2-1B7	CYCYED OCK	LEEVAN TENZA	MAGVA YARRO	EDRIO	SAW GERRERA

SCARIF

This remote tropical planet is home to an Imperial military base with a terrifying secret. The facility is being used to construct a planet-destroying superweapon, the Death Star. Scarif is protected by a deflector shield, but it can be entered through a shield gate ...

JYN CASSIAN BAZE CHIRRUT BODHI KRENNIC

NIIMA OUTPOST

Jakku is an ideal place for scavengers due to its many great shipwrecks from a long-ago battle between the Empire and Rebellion. The ruthless Unkar Plutt has a stronghold on the settlement where these scavengers come to trade their finds.

REY **BB-8** **UNKAR PLUTT** **SARCO PLANK** **LOR SAN TEKKA** **BOBBAJO**

THE ERAVANA

After losing the *Millennium Falcon*, Han and Chewie came into possession of a large heavy freighter and used it to resume their smuggling career. The *Eravana* is not well-armed, nor is it as fast as the *Falcon*, but it does have the space for a lot of strange cargo, including frightening livestock.

FINN   HAN SOLO   TASU LEECH   REY   BALA-TIK   BB-8

MAZ KANATA'S CASTLE

On the planet Takodana lives a pirate queen, who allows smugglers to reside in her ancient castle. Maz has strict rules against violence, so travellers from across the galaxy can find refuge here from bounty hunters and political enemies.

MAZ KANATA · **HAN SOLO** · **CRIMSON CORSAIR** · **GRUMMGAR** · **BAZINE NETAL** · **EMMIE**

STARKILLER BASE

On an ice planet in the unknown regions, the First Order constructs a base of operations for a superweapon capable of destroying entire star systems. The base's vastness hosts the largest deployment of First Order military forces, including stormtroopers, snowtroopers and naval officers.

CAPTAIN PHASMA • GENERAL HUX • KYLO REN • IT-000 • POE DAMERON • SNOKE

RESISTANCE BASE

The Resistance headquarters is surrounded by thick jungle and the command centre is underground, meaning the facility is well concealed from enemy sensors. Multiple hangars hold the Resistance Fleet including the all-important X-wings.

POE DAMERON

ELLO ASTY

GENERAL LEIA

FINN

NIEN NUNB

PZ-4CO

GALACTIC CHECKLIST

These might be a bit harder to find ...

KAMINO CLONING FACILITY

- ◯ Trooper missing his shoes
- ◯ Trooper with artificial eye
- ◯ A protocol droid
- ◯ Kylo Ren's helmet
- ◯ Trooper looking through a periscope
- ◯ Trooper with a beard
- ◯ Flying trooper in red armour
- ◯ Kaminoan riding an aiwha

DROID FACTORY

- ◯ Blue battle droid
- ◯ Discarded assassin droid
- ◯ Exploding battle droid
- ◯ Giant beetle
- ◯ Viceroy Nute Gunray
- ◯ A Twi'lek with a lightsaber
- ◯ Battle droid with different head
- ◯ A three-legged droid

OTOH GUNGA

- ◯ Gungan walking a lobster
- ◯ Colo claw fish
- ◯ Admiral Ackbar
- ◯ Gungan carrying fruit
- ◯ Gungan playing a drum
- ◯ Gungan with a pink waistcoat
- ◯ Kaadu

LOTHAL

- ◯ Group of Quarren
- ◯ Mechanic under speeder
- ◯ Bith inspecting crystals on sale
- ◯ Biths in a window
- ◯ Girl trying on rebel helmet
- ◯ Carpet salesman
- ◯ Brain in a jar
- ◯ Thirsty birds

DOCKING BAY 94

- ○ Barbecue
- ○ Rodian playing a trumpet
- ○ Droid DJ
- ○ A Toong
- ○ Carrots
- ○ X-wing pilot
- ○ Sleeping Ewok
- ○ Two Toydarians

THE PIT OF CARKOON

- ○ Gamorrean caught by the Sarlacc
- ○ Spit roast
- ○ Baby Hutt
- ○ Bossk
- ○ Dewback
- ○ Battering ram
- ○ Salacious Crumb
- ○ Herd of banthas

HOME ONE

- ○ Coffee flask
- ○ Rodian X-wing pilot
- ○ X-wing pilot writing a letter
- ○ Red X-wing pilot helmet
- ○ Death Star hologram
- ○ Air traffic controller
- ○ Aqualish officers
- ○ Droid on outside of ship doing maintenance

JEDHA

- ○ Brown bird
- ○ Brotherhood of the Beatific Countenance
- ○ Red R2 unit
- ○ Tank being pelted with fruit
- ○ Man getting drenched by bucket of water
- ○ Fruit seller
- ○ Man with eye patch
- ○ Alien rebel pilot

SAW GERRERA'S HIDEOUT

- O Partisans playing dejarik
- O Kids trying on trooper helmets
- O Man cutting meat
- O Headless droid
- O Trooper reading a book
- O Young Rodian playing
- O Man examining kyber crystals
- O Nautolan offering bread

SCARIF

- O Rebel with spade
- O Protocol droid soldier
- O Rebel Ewok
- O Rebel on top of palm tree
- O Rebel shooting a rocket launcher
- O Imperial citadel tower

NIIMA OUTPOST

- O Crusher Roodown
- O Rey's stolen speeder
- O Blue BB unit
- O A game of cards
- O Angry one-eyed man
- O Mushroom head
- O Baby Happabore

THE *ERAVANA*

- ☐ Mynocks
- ☐ Mandalorians fighting a rathtar
- ☐ Open can of worms
- ☐ Man riding a green alien
- ☐ Orange R2 unit
- ☐ Blue lightsaber
- ☐ Man caught by wampa
- ☐ Royal Guards

MAZ KANATA'S CASTLE

- ☐ A Mandalorian flag
- ☐ Man who has lost his glasses
- ☐ Droid knocking over some fruit
- ☐ Woman cleaning a statue
- ☐ Thromba and Laparo
- ☐ Pair of eyes staring out of a door
- ☐ A picnic
- ☐ Guavian Death Gang soldiers

STARKILLER BASE

- ☐ Ralph McQuarrie R2-D2
- ☐ Protocol droid
- ☐ Darth Vader's helmet
- ☐ Man hiding in vent
- ☐ Officer enjoying a hot drink
- ☐ TIE fighter on a screen
- ☐ First Order officer with a magnifying glass
- ☐ Wampa prisoner

RESISTANCE BASE

- ☐ B-U4D
- ☐ Officer with a broken arm
- ☐ Blue flight suit
- ☐ Woman sitting on power droid
- ☐ Droid head being repaired
- ☐ Stormtrooper being arrested
- ☐ Alien at the console